World of Reading

2

BATTLE WITH ULTRON

Adapted by Chris "Doc" Wyatt

Illustrated by Andrea Di Vito and Rachelle Rosenberg

Based on the Marvel comic book series The Avengers

ABDO
Spotlight

Los Angeles
New York

ABDOPUBLISHING.COM

Reinforced library bound edition published in 2018 by Spotlight, a division of ABDO, PO Box 398166, Minneapolis, Minnesota 55439. Spotlight produces high-quality reinforced library bound editions for schools and libraries. Published by Marvel Press, an imprint of Disney Book Group.

Printed in the United States of America, North Mankato, Minnesota.
042017
092017

marvelkids.com
© 2015 MARVEL

THIS BOOK CONTAINS
RECYCLED MATERIALS

PUBLISHER'S CATALOGING-IN-PUBLICATION DATA

Names: Wyatt, Chris, author. | Di Vito, Andrea ; Rosenberg, Rachelle, illustrators.
Title: The Avengers: battle with Ultron / writer: Chris Wyatt ; art: Andrea Di Vito ; Rachelle Rosenberg.
Other titles: Battle with Ultron
Description: Reinforced library bound edition. | Minneapolis, Minnesota : Spotlight, 2018. | Series: World of reading level 2
Summary: Iron Man forms a new team of Avengers to save his friends from the evil robot, Ultron.
Identifiers: LCCN 2017936173 | ISBN 9781532140600 (lib. bdg.)
Subjects: LCSH: Avengers (Fictitious characters)--Juvenile fiction. | Superheroes--Juvenile fiction. | Adventure and adventurers--Juvenile fiction. | Comic books, strips, etc.--Juvenile fiction. | Graphic novels--Juvenile fiction.
Classification: DDC [E]--dc23
LC record available at https://lccn.loc.gov/2017936173

Spotlight
A Division of ABDO
abdopublishing.com

Iron Man is in space.
He is fixing a broken satellite.

He returns to Avengers Tower.
It is quiet.

Iron Man looks for his friends.

He checks the security system.
Ultron has captured the Avengers!
Ultron is an evil robot.

Iron Man knows he has
to rescue his friends!

He will need help. He goes off to
find a new team of Super Heroes.

First, he calls Black Widow.
She is a secret agent. She is smart
and good at solving cases.

Next is Hawkeye.
He can hit anything!
Some of his arrows even explode!

Later, they find Falcon.

Falcon is a great fighter.

He can fly like a bird.

Then, they ask Quicksilver.
He can move faster than anything.

Scarlet Witch is Quicksilver's twin
sister. She has magical powers.

Last is Vision. He is an android.
He can pass through walls
and fire laser beams.

Some of Iron Man's friends
agree to help right away.

Some are unsure. They have never
thought of themselves as heroes
before.

Iron Man knows they are strong.
Iron Man knows they are good.
Iron Man knows they can be
Avengers.

Soon they form a new team
of Avengers.

Vision scans the place for clues. He finds footprints! They belong to Ultron and his army of evil robots.

Black Widow uses the S.H.I.E.L.D. database to track Ultron and his army of robots.

When they get to the secret
hideout, Scarlet Witch uses her
magic to sneak them inside.

Bad robots guard the base.
Hawkeye knocks out the robots
without being seen.

Deep inside, they find Ultron.
He did not know they were there!

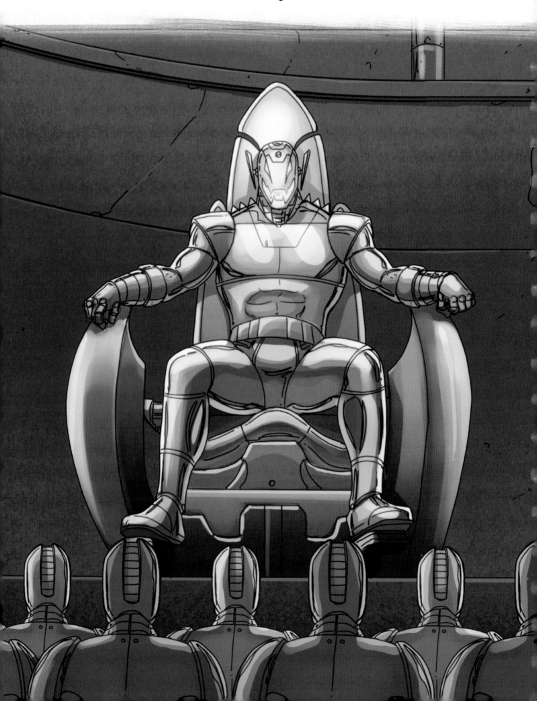

Falcon comes up with a plan.
He will attack Ultron first!

All the new Avengers jump in.
They fight Ultron and his robots.

It is a big battle!

Quicksilver runs past the villains.
He frees the Avengers.

Ultron knows he cannot defeat
them all. He tries to flee.

The old Avengers fight alongside
the new Avengers.

Together, they stop Ultron!

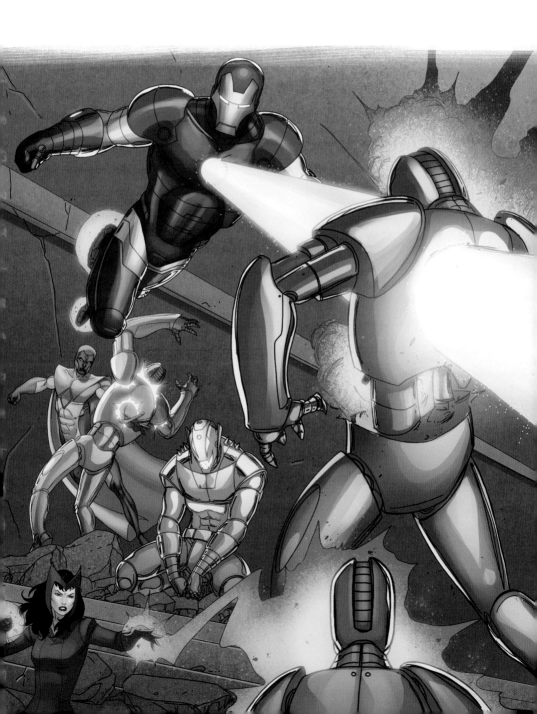

The Avengers thank the new Avengers. They decide to team up for many more adventures!